For my amazing family and all the chicks that inspired this story. ~ K.A.G.

For my Grandad. ~ R.S.

GNOME ROAD PUBLISHING
Louisville, Kentucky, USA
www.gnomeroadpublishing.com
Logo designs by Wendy Leach, Copyright © 2023 by Gnome Road Publishing

Summary: When your chickens start begging for books, you'll know it's time to
teach them to read! Find a cozy place to rest their chicken cheeks,
then help them peck the right story. Readers don't hatch overnight,
but with your help, words will begin flying off the pages.

ISBN 978-1-957655-05-5 (trade) | ISBN 978-1-957655-12-3 (ebook)
Library of Congress Control Number: 2022939016
LC record available at: https://lccn.loc.gov/2022939016

Illustrations were rendered using a mixture
of digital, pencil, and scanned textures.
The text of this book is set in Gitan Latin.

First Edition
10 9 8 7 6 5 4 3 2 1
Manufactured in India

How to Hatch a Reader

Kari Ann Gonzalez   Rachel Suzanne

Are your chickens begging for b-b-b-book, books?
If so, it is time to teach your feathered friends to read.

But first . . .

. . . you have
to catch them!

Once they are calm, find a cozy place to rest their chicken cheeks. Then practice letter sounds.

"A" for apple.

"B" for bugs.

"C" for coop.

"D" for dirt.

"E" for eggs.

"F" for . . . FOX!

BUWACK!

Just kidding, chickens.

When they are ready, start pointing out common words.

Then let your chickens discover their own.

Next, help them label their favorite things.
Encourage every chicken scratch!

Once they have the basics, help your chickens peck interesting stories to read. Flip the pages to let them discover...

a fabulous farm,

a dancing dinosaur,

a caped underwear
crusader, or ...

Sorry chickens!
Best to avoid scary stories,

and . . .
FOWL language.

Next, try sounding out the words.

D-U-C-K

Your turn chickens.

C-L-U-C-K

T-R-U-C-K

Try this one, chickens.

One more, chickens … **P-L-U-C-K**

Just kidding, chickens.
Last try . . .

C-L-U-C-K

C-L-U-C-K

EGG-cellent, chickens!

Before you know it, paired words
will roll right off their tongues.

Book-worm.

Bird-seed.

Shake your **tail-feathers.**

Now celebrate with a dance party . . .

Reading whole sentences is tough. Remind your chickens to keep their eye on the prize. After all, readers don't hatch overnight!

Soon, words will fly off the pages, and reading will open up a world of possibilities.

Watch out for that …

.... FOX?

Careful, the sky is falling!

Or is it?

The fox must like
your books, chickens!
You know what to do.

How
to
Hatch a
Reader
- - - - -

What are you reading now, chickens?

Learning to read can be fun! So can teaching others. If you know someone special who is ready to read, here are a few ways to get started.

1) Read together out loud, every day.

2) Practice letter sounds.

3) Point out common words.

4) Help your reader label their favorite things.

5) Sound out words together.

6) When you get to tricky words, try word-attack strategies:
   - Slowly s-t-r-e-t-c-h out the letter sounds.
   - Look for chunks of words you know.
   - Look for clues in the picture.

7) Ask questions at key page turns:
   - What do you think will happen next?
   - What would you have done?

8) At the end of the story ask a few more fun questions:
   - What was your favorite part of the story?
   - Do you know a friend that might like this book? Why?

9) Act out the story after reading it or just your favorite scenes.

10) Celebrate every milestone!

For additional information, you can visit:

https://www2.ed.gov/parents/read/resources/edpicks.jhtml

https://www.readingrockets.org/blogs/right-read/abcs-teaching-reading-home

https://readingpartners.org/take-action/resources-for-families/

About the Author: Kari Ann Gonzalez is a writer of children's fiction and informational fiction with a heaping helping of humor and STEAM concepts. When she is not regaling her family with tall tales or creating colorful characters for her stories, you will find her reading voraciously. Two cats and six chickens are kind enough to share their home with Kari and her family in California. To learn more about Kari, visit her website at: www.kurianngonzalez.com.

About the Illustrator: Rachel Suzanne graduated from Birmingham City University, England with First class honours in Illustration. She enjoys creating work through crossing digital art with traditional medium, especially experimental mark making. When she's not drawing, she's likely to be in a theatre. Learn more about Rachel by visiting her website at: www.rachelsuzanne.com.

For additional materials, including a free resource guide for parents and educators, please visit us at: www.gnomeroadpublishing.com.